Postcards From Stella Maris

Also by Susan M. Boyer

Lowcountry Boil (A Liz Talbot Mystery, Book 1)

Lowcountry Bombshell (A Liz Talbot Mystery, Book 2)

Lowcountry Boneyard (A Liz Talbot Mystery, Book 3)

Lowcountry Bordello (A Liz Talbot Mystery, Book 4)

Lowcountry Book Club (A Liz Talbot Mystery, Book 5)

Lowcountry Bonfire (A Liz Talbot Mystery, Book 6)

Lowcountry Bookshop (A Liz Talbot Mystery, Book 7)

Lowcountry Boomerang (A Liz Talbot Mystery, Book 8)

Lowcountry Boondoggle (A Liz Talbot Mystery, Book 9)

Lowcountry Boughs of Holly (A Liz Talbot Mystery, Book 10)

Coming Soon! Lowcountry Getaway (A Liz Talbot Mystery, Book 11)

Postcards From Stella Maris

FIVE LIZ TALBOT SHORT STORIES

SUSAN M. BOYER

STELLA MARIS BOOKS
LLC

"Hogwash" originally appeared in *Spinetingler Magazine, Winter 2006, Issue #10* Copyright © 2005 by Susan M. Boyer

"Highlights & Hot Lead" originally appeared in *Catfish Stew, Volume IV, 2006,* Copyright © 2005 by Susan M. Boyer

"Everything is Relative" originally appeared in *The Petigru Review, Volume 1, 2007,* Copyright © 2006 by Susan M. Boyer

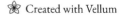 Created with Vellum

About these stories...

These stories are for fans of the Liz Talbot Mystery series. They are snapshots of life on Stella Maris, the island where Liz Talbot lives. If you've never read a Liz Talbot mystery novel, I would encourage you to start with *Lowcountry Boil (A Liz Talbot Mystery, Book 1)* and come back to these short stories later.

I believe these stories will be most enjoyed by readers who are familiar with the characters and setting. I wrote the stories as I was developing the characters. Because the stories deal with things that happened in the characters' backgrounds that helped shaped their lives, the tone is sometimes quite different from the tone of the novels themselves. Some of the stories have been previously published in journals, and others have never before been published.

I so hope you enjoy these glimpses into Liz Talbot's formative years, her unfortunate first marriage, and her life between major cases.

Warmly,

Susan M. Boyer

For MaryAnn, who does All the Things...

Postcards From Stella Maris

Common Knowledge

September 1986

Colleen sprang backward, launching all sixty-five pounds of herself into the big swing on Liz's screened porch.

Liz squealed. "It's going crooked!"

"But we're swinging now!" Colleen grabbed the chain and stretched her legs out as the swing arced toward the ceiling. "Help me!"

Both girls tucked their legs and leaned into the motion, driving the swing higher. They giggled, raised their palms for a high-five, and settled in for the ride.

"How many things do you have that start with 'c?'" Liz asked.

"None, yet," Colleen said. "I have to do it at my house."

Liz dipped her chin, raised her eyebrows, and wagged the end of her ponytail at Colleen. "Mrs. Ravenel didn't say that."

"Oh yes, she did." Colleen always listened like her Mamma taught her—once with her ears, and once with her head. "Besides, if we both find things in your backyard that start with 'c,' we'll have all the same answers."

"Fine." Liz rolled her eyes. They swung up and back, up and back. "I'm glad we both got Mrs. Ravenel."

"Me, too." Colleen grinned. "Is it almost time for dinner?"

Liz looked through the window into the kitchen. "Probably. What are you going to tell about your summer?"

"Camping out on the beach and making s'mores. What are you telling about?"

"Our new house," Liz said. "And Marci."

"What's Marci got to do with your new house?"

Liz moved the big flowered pillow to the side of the swing, smacked it twice, and leaned back against it so that she faced Colleen. She stretched out her legs on the swing and crossed her ankles. "My second favorite thing about the new house is that Marci and Aunt Sharon and Uncle Paul don't live here."

Colleen laughed.

Liz's big brother, Blake, walked across the backyard and opened the screen door. "Colleen, you laugh like a donkey-pig, and you look like Little Orphan Annie, only fatter."

Liz jumped down from the swing. She stumbled and almost fell on the brick floor. Steadying herself, she squinted hard at Blake. "Take it back."

"Will not," he said.

Liz propped her fists on her hips and leaned towards him. "You take it back right this minute."

"You can't make me."

"Mamma!" Liz shouted. She bolted for the door leading to the kitchen.

Blake followed her inside, and Colleen trailed behind swiping at the tears on her cheeks. Why couldn't Blake and the other boys like her? Blake was one year older than Colleen and Liz. He'd started second grade that day. But he played with the boys in Liz and Colleen's class, and they always made fun of her. Lots of times they picked on her and Liz both, calling them names like "Cream Puff Annies," and "The Two Little Piglets." Liz was what Colleen's Mamma called "pleasingly plump." Colleen was fat.

"Mammmma!" Liz called again.

"Lard-Bottom Tattletale." Blake grabbed a cookie from the jar and slipped back out through the porch.

"What's going on in here?" Mrs. Talbot walked in from the family room.

Liz pointed at the door. "Blake said Colleen laughs like a donkey-pig and looks like Little Orphan Annie, only fatter."

Mrs. Talbot hurried to Colleen's side, crouched beside her, and hugged her tight. "Sweetheart, you can't pay any attention to silly ole boys. In a few years, they'll be changing their story, you mark my words." She cradled Colleen's face in one hand and smoothed her hair with the other. "You have the prettiest red curls I've ever seen. And your eyes are beautiful—the color of my grandmother's emerald ring."

Colleen sniffled hard, trying to breathe Mrs. Talbot in. She always smelled like the purple flowers in Colleen's mamma's garden.

"Blake's not getting any chocolate cake, right, Mamma?" Liz climbed onto a bar stool.

Colleen's spirits lifted. "There's chocolate cake?"

Mrs. Talbot laughed. "Yes, I made one this afternoon. And you can have as big a slice as you like."

"My mamma only lets me have sweets on special occasions. I have to watch my figure," Colleen said.

Mrs. Talbot moved to the stove and stirred the spaghetti sauce. It smelled so good it was making Colleen's stomach growl. "Well, I'm sure she counts your first day of first grade as a special occasion. I bet she would have baked a cake herself if she didn't have to work in the hardware store today."

"Do you really think so?" Colleen asked. Her mamma almost never baked cakes.

"Of course," Mrs. Talbot said. She walked back into the family room, calling over her shoulder. "I'm going to check on the baby. Dinner will be ready in half an hour."

"What's your first favorite thing about the new house?"

3

Colleen asked. She'd overheard her mamma say it was tastefully decorated for something so ridiculously large.

"I don't have to share a room with Marci. She's mean and weird."

"I thought that was your second favorite thing," Colleen said.

"I guess it's my first and my second favorite thing."

"Mine too. I hate Marci. She tells us we're babies eighty-zillion times a day, and she's only two years older."

"I miss you living right across the street, though." Liz bit her lip.

"Me too." Colleen picked up the box of spaghetti on the bar and shook it back and forth.

Liz's mamma came back into the kitchen. "I'm going to set the table, girls. Get washed up for dinner." She smiled and caressed Liz's shoulder as she passed behind her on the way into the dining room.

Liz climbed down from the bar stool, and she and Colleen raced down the hall to the powder room. Colleen reached for the bottle of hand soap. Her own mamma wouldn't buy soap in a bottle because it was something called "an extravagance." Colleen loved the smell of it—it smelled almost as good as Liz's mamma—and the strangeness of it. She always pumped some for Liz, then herself. Liz always let her. Liz could pump soap from a bottle any time. They rubbed their hands together, making a pile of bubbles in the sink.

The front doorbell chimed.

"Carolyn, someone's at the door," Mr. Talbot called from the family room. At Colleen's house, they didn't have a family room. They had a living room, a library, and her daddy's study—but no family room.

The front door opened. A few minutes passed, then it closed. Loud voices came from the family room. Colleen glanced at Liz. She was scrubbing her hands so hard they were red.

Mrs. Talbot sounded really mad. "It's Ponder. I have told you before, I will not have him in my house. This is our home. It is not some bar."

"Carolyn—"

"What will the neighbors think? Everyone knows he's a drunk. I will not expose my children to the likes of him."

"I didn't invite him here," Mr. Talbot said.

"If Colleen's parents knew he was coming around, why they'd never let her come back. Do you want our children to be ostracized, Franklin? I notice he never came knocking at your mother's door."

Colleen wondered what ostracized meant. She'd seen an ostrich on television the week before. Would Liz get to have one of those big birds for a pet?

Liz looked up without moving her head. Colleen's eyes locked with hers.

"Is he still out there, Carolyn?" Mr. Talbot's voice sounded aggravated, but he wasn't yelling like Mrs. Talbot.

"He's standing on the front porch. He wants to talk to you."

"I'll give him a bottle of liquor, then he'll leave, okay? He's just craving a drink and probably broke."

"As long as you keep giving him booze, he'll keep coming back. People will think we're just like him...trash."

Liz's baby sister, Merry, started crying.

"He's my cousin, Carolyn. Everybody already knows that, whether he comes around or not. Nobody holds his drinking against you."

A cabinet door opened and slammed closed. Then the front door opened and closed again.

Colleen grabbed Liz's soapy hands with hers. "I'll never tell."

Fat teardrops slid down Liz's cheeks. "Best friends forever?"

"And ever and ever," said Colleen.

July 1989

. . .

The space underneath Gram's deck made a great clubhouse. Colleen and Liz built walls with lounge chairs turned on their sides. This was their favorite place to retreat with a quilt and Nancy Drew when Liz's mamma had errands to run and they needed to stay out from underneath Colleen's mamma's feet. Gram never minded them being under her feet—or her deck. She always had homemade fried apple pies, cream puffs, or chocolate chip cookies on hand for them.

That afternoon, they'd been reading for an hour when they heard footsteps on the deck above them. Next came the sounds of chairs being adjusted and drinks being placed on the table between them. The smell of cigarette smoke drifted down into the clubhouse. Both girls wrinkled their faces and pinched their noses.

Then they heard Liz's aunt Sharon's scratchy voice. "This beats the hell out of that dinky little patio at the house."

"Well, yeah, it's right on the ocean. Shit, Sharon, why didn't you and Paul stay here? Why in hell would you move into that tiny little rental when you could've stayed here for free?" Aunt Sharon's friend Tiffany asked.

Colleen pressed both hands over her mouth to hold the giggles in. She'd never heard that many cuss words at one time in her whole life.

"Paul hated it here—always under Daddy's thumb, living by their rules."

"Yeah, that would suck," Tiffany said.

Liz put down her book, rolled over, and flopped on her back. She stared through the decking at her aunt Sharon. Colleen's giggles disappeared.

"And I think Mamma and Daddy were ready for an empty nest. We weren't even here a year, but Frank and Carolyn had been here for over six," Aunt Sharon said.

"Looks to me like you and Paul got the short end of that deal. Miss high-and-mighty Carolyn gets herself a brand new, five-bedroom, two-story house, and you get stuck in that closet-sized rattrap."

Liz's eyes got all squinty and mean. She grabbed fistfuls of the quilt.

"Frank busted his ass going to college and working full-time for six years. And trust me, in Mamma and Daddy's house, they were six long years of living right. Saved his money—I don't begrudge him the nice house."

"Yeah, whatever," said Tiffany.

"And Carolyn's not so bad. I feel kinda sorry for her. She was first in her class, could have gone to college...been somebody. Hell, she married Frank for the same reason Paul married me."

"No shit?"

"My daddy put his foot down and that was that. She'd have been a lot better off if she'd had an abortion and gone on to college. That little brat of hers ruined her life. And now look at her...three kids in five years. She's nothing but a baby machine, pumping out little Talbots."

Colleen jumped up and bolted out from beneath the deck towards the front of the house, dragging Liz along behind her. Neither of them spoke until they had crossed the street and climbed the steps to Colleen's front porch.

Liz's lower lip trembled, her face streaked with tears. "What's an a-a-ab-abortion?"

Colleen put her arm around her friend. "I don't know, but we can ask Deanna." Colleen's sister Deanna was five years older than Liz and Colleen and a trusted authority on most subjects. "I think she's upstairs in her room reading."

Colleen opened the front door, and they ran across the foyer and straight up the stairs. Colleen hesitated at Deanna's door, fist poised to knock. An abortion couldn't be anything good. Maybe they didn't want to know.

"Knock!" Liz said.

Colleen knocked, but not very hard.

Deanna opened the door. She held a book in her hand, but

she didn't look mad the way a lot of big sisters would if you interrupted them while they were reading. "What's up?" she asked.

Colleen's eyes pled with her sister to make everything all right.

Deanna opened the door wider and stepped back to let them in. She crossed the room and hopped up on her bed amongst a pile of pillows. She patted the bed in front of her. "Come on up."

The girls climbed up and settled cross-legged on the bed. Liz grabbed a pillow and hugged it to her chest, rocking back and forth. Colleen looked at Liz, then at Deanna.

Without looking up, Liz asked, "What's an abortion?"

Deanna's eyes widened. "Where did you hear that word?"

"From Tiffany Shuping," Colleen said.

Deanna's shoulders rose and fell as she puffed out a breath that fluttered through her bangs. "Well," she said, "I guess you have to learn about this sometime. And since some people of low breeding don't know to watch what they say—"

"De-*anna*..." Colleen jiggled her leg.

Deanna cleared her throat. "I overheard Mother and some of the ladies from the church discussing it after bible study."

"But what does it mean?" Liz asked.

"An abortion is when a woman chooses to end her pregnancy," Deanna said solemnly.

"You mean—?" Colleen squinted at her sister.

"I mean she doesn't carry the baby to term," said Deanna. "Look, this is really pretty complicated. Not something the two of you need to be worried about at all. I shouldn't have...how about some ice cream?"

Colleen wrapped her arms around Liz, the way she'd seen Liz's mamma do so many times. Why would Liz's stupid Aunt Sharon think that Mrs. Talbot should have stopped being pregnant with Blake and gone to college? What would've happened to Blake?

Liz whispered in her ear, "Never tell."

"Never," said Colleen.

October 1994

Carolyn sat beside Liz on the sofa in the family room, one arm draped around her daughter. She smoothed Liz's hair. She really had blossomed in the last year. She'd grown several inches, lost a few pounds, and redistributed a few others. Liz was quite a striking young lady.

"Of course, you should go," Carolyn said.

"But Colleen and I have already made plans to go to the sock hop together." Liz stared at the fireplace.

"Sweetheart, you know how much I think of Colleen." She wrapped Liz in both arms and squeezed. "But don't you think it would be a good idea to cultivate other friendships as well?"

"I have other friends. But Colleen is my best friend."

"But Olivia Beauthorpe and Sarabeth Rivers...well, they come from such good families. They are quite popular, aren't they?" Carolyn asked.

"Yes, Mamma, and I do like them. I have four classes with Courtney and three with Sarabeth, and I'm glad they invited me to the sock hop and slumber party. It's just that—"

"I'm not saying you shouldn't still be friends with Colleen, of course, you should—Colleen will always be your friend."

"Colleen is my best friend." Liz crossed her arms.

"But when you have the opportunity to socialize with the other girls, I don't think you should say no just because Colleen won't be there. I don't want you to limit yourself, is all." Carolyn sighed. Colleen was stuck in that awkward stage, and she had such unfortunate skin, the poor dear.

Carolyn knew it sounded shallow to Liz, but she wanted her daughter to be happy, and having the right group of friends was the key to happiness as one approached high school years. Hers were still very fresh in her memory.

9

"When I first met your daddy, I was a cheerleader and on student council..." Carolyn wrapped both arms around Liz, pulled her close, and held her there. She rested her chin on top of Liz's head. "Who knows? If I'd gone on to college like I planned, I might have been a USC cheerleader."

The grandfather clock in the foyer announced the arrival of five o'clock.

Liz sighed. "All right, Mamma."

June 1997

Colleen dialed the phone and stared out her window as it rang. The giant white house across the street called to her. With all her heart, Colleen wanted to run over there, crawl underneath the deck, and be seven again.

Liz answered on the fourth ring.

"Hey, what's up?" Colleen said. She reached for a perky tone and hoped she'd managed something north of gloomy.

"It is so good to hear from you!" Liz said. "I haven't talked to you in forever! So tell me...what have you been up to?" She had mastered perky a few years back.

"Oh, you know. The usual. I stay busy." Colleen prayed her voice didn't betray how desperately she was trying to sound upbeat. She drew a ragged breath and plunged ahead. "Hey, how about we catch a movie tonight? We haven't done that in ages, and I'm dying to see *Men in Black*."

"Oh, gosh, I'm so sorry Colleen. I'd love to, but Jackson and I are double-dating tonight with Sarabeth and Tommy."

Colleen imagined what was likely happening on the other end of the line: Liz bit her lip and cringed, as she ran perfectly manicured nails through professionally-highlighted blonde hair. Liz would know that the reason she couldn't go to the movies would be more hurtful to Colleen than the fact that she couldn't go. It was common knowledge that at seventeen, Colleen had never been on a date.

"Hey, no problem...I know how it is," Colleen said. "We'll do it another time."

"Absolutely." Liz sighed. "Colleen...I can't believe it's been so long. Things have just been so crazy..."

Colleen knew Liz was sincere, but would be hard pressed to find an open date on her calendar. Between Jackson, cheerleading practice, class officer meetings, and her family, Liz was likely booked into the next decade.

Colleen let her off the hook. "Listen, I hate to run, but I really have to go. Mom is expecting a call from Deanna and Adam—they're still on their honeymoon—and she's jumping up and down for me to get off the phone."

"Sure...I understand. Promise you'll call me back as soon as you get a chance?"

"Okay...sure," Colleen promised.

"I miss you, Colleen." Liz's voice was wistful.

"I miss you, too." Colleen closed her eyes.

"I'll talk to you soon, then. Bye now."

Liz's words seared Colleen's heart. She barely managed to form a reply. "Bye, Liz."

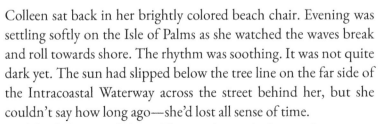

Colleen sat back in her brightly colored beach chair. Evening was settling softly on the Isle of Palms as she watched the waves break and roll towards shore. The rhythm was soothing. It was not quite dark yet. The sun had slipped below the tree line on the far side of the Intracoastal Waterway across the street behind her, but she couldn't say how long ago—she'd lost all sense of time.

The light was fading. The sun-lovers had gone hours ago, followed by the late afternoon walkers with their various breeds of dogs and the after-work kite-flyers. The last few fishermen on the beach were packing up their tackle boxes to head home for supper. She took a long drink from the jumbo pink plastic drink cup that she'd brought along. She grimaced. What did people see in this stuff? She must have poured too much tequila and not enough margarita mix.

The hardest part of executing her revised plans for that Friday night had been getting the tequila. One thing you would never find in the Stevens' home was alcohol of any description—aside from the kind you put on cuts. But for a five-dollar tip, Sam Manigault, who had just turned twenty-one, had agreed to buy it for her. Then, she'd packed up her beach chair in the trunk of the gray Honda Accord she'd shared with her sister since she'd turned sixteen and took the ferry over to the Isle of Palms.

A family of seagulls sailed over her head. If only she could fly away, to anywhere but here. If only she could be someone else... anyone else. Colleen sighed and downed half of the remaining toxic brew in her cup, spilling some on her bathing suit cover-up in the process. It didn't matter.

She wasn't mad at Liz for not being free to go to the movies with her—she'd known that Liz would have plans on a Friday night—she was one of the most popular girls at Stella Maris High School, and she'd been dating Jackson Beauthorpe for almost a year. She missed Liz. Even though they hadn't spent any real time together in years, Colleen still thought of Liz as her best friend. *You're pathetic*, she sneered at herself. *Calling Liz was stupid. Now she knows you're pathetic too.*

Colleen shrugged. That didn't matter, either.

She wasn't mad at Deanna for getting married and leaving her alone in the house with their psychotically protective parents. Colleen peered into the future and saw the dismal certainty that she would now be the focus of their unrelenting love and concern, Deanna having successfully landed an eminently suitable husband. She would miss her sister, although Deanna wasn't moving away like some girls did after they got married. She would live within a few miles of the house they grew up in, but things would never be the same. Colleen's aloneness would be unmitigated by her sister's effervescent presence in the house.

She wasn't mad at her parents, only weary of trying to blossom into something that they could be content—if not completely satisfied—with. Colleen sympathized with them—she wasn't happy with who she was in the least. But her parents' endless efforts to improve her, and her mother's resentment of the related expenditures, which she insisted on making, had worn Colleen down. The psychologist was the last straw.

She had endured the teeth straightening and whitening, the bi-weekly visits to the dermatologist with the attendant parade of lotions and creams which never seemed to have the advertised effect on her skin, the countless diets and exercise programs, and even the modeling lessons—she wondered how they had taken her mother's money with a straight face—designed to give her poise. But when they tried to make her discuss her inadequacies with a stranger once a week, she gave up.

Finally, Colleen was alone on the beach in the twilight. She chugged the rest of her drink, then sat her cup down in the sand. Unsteadily, she pulled herself to her feet, slipped out of her cover-up, and strolled towards the water, eyes furtively scanning the beach. If anyone had seen her, they would have noticed she was weaving rather dramatically. Colleen had never had alcohol before, and she had ingested half a bottle of tequila in the last two hours. She was dizzy and a little queasy.

The horizon tipped. She giggled and spread her arms wide for balance. Near the surf, she made a hard right turn and ran alongside the water, leaning right, then left, soaring like the seagulls she so desperately envied. She flew alongside the water as the beach turned inward and ran back up Breach Inlet towards the bridge.

The skull and crossbones on the warning signs prominently displayed on both sides of the inlet always made her shiver, and this evening was no different. Colleen stopped abruptly and stared at the water. Dozens of people had drowned here. The waters that flowed between the Isle of Palms and Sullivan's Island were treacherous, the current swift. College kids sometimes tried to swim across on a bet. Some of them made it to the other side, exhilarated at having cheated the powerful, sucking tide of its rightful bounty. Others lost much more than their money.

Colleen took off her tennis shoes. She briefly considered undressing completely, just to feel the water against her skin—she'd never been skinny-dipping. There were a great many things she had never done. Her mother's face flashed before her eyes and she decided to leave her swimsuit on. There were limits to what she was willing to put her family through to buy her freedom.

With a running start, Colleen dove into the dark water.

The next day, when they found her, her death would be ruled accidental. This would be easier for her family to accept, but utterly wrong.

Eviction

April 2009
  Greenville, South Carolina

Liz glared over the screen of her laptop at the stranger standing in her kitchen doorway. His features were familiar—she'd been married to him for eight years. The professionally trained body, golf course suntan, and chemically whitened teeth were those of her husband, no doubt about it. But she found no trace of recognition in the soul inhabiting the body. It was as if the mothership had sucked the life force out of Scott Andrews while he slept one night and replaced it with one of those aliens incapable of comprehending human emotions. The only question in her mind was why it had taken her so long to realize what had happened.

The puppy he was holding seemed to sense that Scott was more foe than friend. He squirmed to escape the large hands that held him posed next to Scott's imitation of an appealing grin.

"Look at him, Liz—he's adorable. How can you say no to this face? He's full-blooded Golden Retriever. I have the papers and everything. His bloodlines are impeccable."

Liz rolled her cobalt blue eyes slowly across the ceiling and took a deep breath. "I have no doubt. Sturgis Pettigru would never allow any stud that wasn't canine royalty near his precious Victoria." Sturgis Pettigru was the managing partner in the prestigious Greenville investment firm that had recruited Scott fresh out of college. Scott was eager as a sailor on his first night of shore leave to bond with him and had suddenly developed a keen interest in Golden Retrievers when one of the assistants had mentioned in passing that Sturgis and his wife bred them.

It was 9:30 on a Thursday night. Florentine Chicken and Pasta was drying out in the commercial grade oven where Liz kept it warm. She'd given up and eaten alone at the granite island in their Tuscan-inspired kitchen an hour ago. Now, logged onto a subscription database, she'd been engrossed in an adoption-related background search for a client. That is, until Scott came bouncing in the backdoor of their recently renovated 1930s Earle street cottage with his surprise.

Liz tilted her head and raised her left eyebrow. "You work seventy hours a week and I work sixty. When you're not at work, you're at the gym or playing golf with any partner who mentions it within earshot or dragging me to some occasion where the right people are congregating. *Who* is going to take care of this dog?" she demanded, aware of the surge of bottled-up resentment rising towards the surface.

"I will." Scott's voice iced over the way it did now any time she failed to embrace whatever transparent scheme he devised to break out of the pack at Pettigru-Walker Investments.

It repulsed her that he was willing to use a puppy to further his career. "I wasn't aware that you wanted a dog. You never mentioned it." Liz leaned back in the high-backed bar stool, arms crossed. "Have you ever had a dog? In your entire life—any kind of a pet?"

He sat the wiggling puppy on the floor at his feet, avoiding her gaze. "You know I haven't...but I think it's high time, don't you? He won't be any trouble, will you, boy?"

"That's not the point." She raked both sets of fingers through her multi-toned blonde hair until they met at the crown of her head, then leaned back, resting her head in her hands and staring through the ceiling and up into the Heavens in a silent prayer for guidance.

Scott raised his voice several decibels. "Well for God's sake what is it? Why is this such a big damn deal? Everybody has pets... why can't we?"

Liz sighed. "The point is, the only reason you brought that puppy home was to make Sturgis believe that the two of you had a common passion for dogs—a lie."

"That's not true. I've always wanted a dog." His stony glare told her that he intended to stick with this convenient fabrication.

"You have marginally more interest in that dog than you do in taking up water ballet. Pets require time and attention beyond just putting out food and water. You don't even have time for a wife anymore. How can you have time for a dog?"

"Here we go with this again."

The warm, wet stream tinkling down on his foot grabbed his attention. "Ahh...shit! He peed on my Cole Haans. You little shit." Scott jerked his soiled loafer up and reflexively kicked the puppy. "Bad dog!"

The puppy let out a string of loud yelps as it flew across the kitchen.

Liz snapped.

After months of watching her marriage circle the drain, she recognized the sound of the final chug-chug-chug as it made its way into the sewer system. She jumped up from the counter, crossed the room in two strides, and scooped up the whimpering pup. "All right," she said, cuddling the golden ball of fur close. "You win. The dog can stay." The puppy glanced up at her hopefully, sensing that he had found a safe harbor.

Scott looked up from his expensive, damp shoe and the splash of doggy piddle on his pants leg and scowled. He stank.

Liz grabbed her shoulder bag, slung it over her left arm, and rummaged for her keys with the same hand as she headed towards the door, the puppy cradled protectively in the crook of her right arm. She would call Foster Erwin from her cell phone in the car. He was the meanest sonavabitch divorce attorney in Greenville—no doubt, he could tell her the quickest way to get rid of the sonavabitch in her kitchen.

Scott looked from the puddle on the floor, to his soiled pants and shoes, then gaped after Liz in shock as she brushed by him.

"Where are you going?" he asked. "Aren't you going to help me clean this mess up?"

She stopped, one hand on the doorknob, and turned slowly back to pierce him with the death rays shooting from her eyes. Seeing him standing there, with his trademark petulant expression, knowing that he fully expected her to clean up the mess on the floor, clean his shoes, and promptly forget the fact that he had just kicked a helpless puppy, she was certain of one thing: There was no way she was spending another night in the same house with this jerk.

"I," she informed him, "am going to buy a dog bed, some toys, and some dog food." She grinned wickedly at his shoes. "And a book on house training. I'll probably be gone about an hour."

Thinking he had somehow gotten his way, he started to relax.

She quickly corrected his mistake. "When I get back, I expect you to be gone, along with anything that you want from this house. Anything you can haul out in an hour, you can have." She stared him down and let the words sink in.

"Now wait just a damn minute—"

"The dog stays with me. If you are not gone when we get back, I will return him to Sturgis Pettigru and explain that the puppy is not safe in this house as long as you live here. I will describe in graphic detail the incident I just witnessed. Are we clear?"

"Liz, come on now, you can't be—"

"Serious? Don't try me."

"Please spare me the histrionics. I'm too tired—"

"You'd better start packing. Oh, and make sure you clean up that mess before you go."

With that, she slammed the door behind her and left.

Hogwash

I was thirty-four years old when it came to me that life is one big masquerade ball, with all of the guests carefully concealing their true selves behind elaborate disguises. Some of us dance so gracefully in our costumes that no one ever suspects that they only see what we allow. Now, you're probably saying to yourself, "I figured that out by the time I was, oh, about...twelve." I always have been a late bloomer.

Looking back, I guess the epiphany had been pushing towards the surface for a while. I had quite a few hints—a series of incidents where people close to me let their masks slip. But it all became crystal clear the spring I saw Zeke Lyerly, a man I would have sworn I knew, for the first time.

Like so many things in my life, it all started with my daddy.

Before she would let Daddy retire, Mamma insisted that he find something to occupy his time besides sandpapering her nerves all day. Since his two favorite pastimes were haunting flea markets and cussin' at the stock reports on MSNBC, we all put our heads together and came up with the idea for Talbot's Treasures.

It was an old red barn several miles from Mamma's house that we renovated and air-conditioned to the point that you could have hung meat in there. Daddy didn't like to sweat. To help pay the outrageous electricity bills, he rented booths to a few of his cronies and the occasional bored housewife. Near the front door, he sat vigil over the stock ticker, surfed the World Wide Web, and occasionally sold junk.

I went by the flea market one morning late that March to see about Daddy.

"Mornin', Tutti," he called out, not taking his eyes off the television.

Apparently, he had trouble recalling the name they'd put on my birth certificate—Elizabeth—because I never once heard him use it. Tutti was the latest in a long succession of nicknames that came from the vast, unknown frontiers of my daddy's brain. It wasn't just me. Daddy never called anyone by the name their mamma gave them, or anything that sounded remotely like it.

I hugged his neck, careful not to muss his hair. He looked much younger than his fifty-two years and was quite vain. There wasn't a single gray hair in his sandy blond head, which was the exact same color as mine before Phoebe—the town's best beautician and best-loved Yankee transplant—added my multi-toned highlights.

"Hey, Daddy. How are you feeling this morning? Mamma says your blood pressure's up."

"The whistle pigs got into your mamma's bulbs again last night," he said, eyes still glued to the stock ticker.

The island off the coast of South Carolina where we lived had a thriving herd of wild hogs. In the aftermath of some hurricane or other back in the 1800s, most of the livestock wandered the island until fences and barns were repaired or rebuilt. This particular gang of hogs was never apprehended. Daddy called them whistle pigs—don't ask me why. I was pretty sure that whistle pig was technically another name for a woodchuck, but Daddy never was much troubled by technicalities. Anyway, as far as I knew, no one had ever heard one of the hogs whistle.

Now, I generally considered these hogs mostly harmless. That said, they liked to snack on delicacies found in flowerbeds and vegetable gardens, which made them unpopular among the human residents of the island. It's my understanding that feral hogs are widely considered by the experts in such matters to be a danger to humans, pets, and biodiversity, due to their predatory nature, the pathogens they harbor, and the fact that they have no natural predators themselves. Also, apparently, they're responsible for millions of dollars in crop damages in other places, but I digress. It wasn't clear to me from Daddy's response whether the hogs had his blood pressure up, or if it was something on the stock ticker.

"Those things are a menace," I said. The idea of hogs running loose had always bothered me a bit if I'm honest. I harbored the suspicion that one of them might attack somebody, although I'd never heard of such a thing happening, at least not in Stella Maris. There had been a lot of discussion regarding what to do about the infestation, but no consensus was reached. Several of the island's matriarchs were too tenderhearted to hear tell of the hogs being exterminated, and the swine were wily enough to evade all efforts at rounding them up.

I noticed Tammy Sue Lyerly frantically trying to get my attention from across the barn. Tammy Sue had a booth in the flea market where she sold such handmade items as purses, appliquéd sweatshirts, and inspirational cross-stitched home décor. Since Daddy was preoccupied and unlikely to move from his recliner, I went on over to see what had Tammy Sue so worked up.

She grabbed a hold of my arm like it was a branch extended to her while she dangled from the side of a cliff. Her other arm clutched her ample chest, and her eyes, round with import, darted from side to side, as if to make sure that no one was eavesdropping. It was only 8:30. The only other occupants of the barn were my daddy and his Basset hound, who were both oblivious.

"*Liz!* Am I glad to see you," she said.

"Tammy Sue, what on earth is wrong?" I asked.

She was wound so tight, for a moment she couldn't get the

words out. She just stood there, clutching my arm and her bosom for dear life and shaking the biggest head of long red hair anybody's seen since 1980. Then, in a stage whisper, she told me, "I am in need of your services. In a *professional* capacity."

Back then, I was the only private investigator on the island. There really wasn't much to investigate in my hometown—most of my business came from old-money Charleston. Within our palm tree and live oak-lined streets, everybody loved secrets so much that their first instinct was to share them over iced tea on the front porch, making it impossible to hide anything. This made it unusual for anybody local to need my services. I was intrigued.

"What's going on?" I asked her.

Her chest began to heave in little spasms. I thought for a moment she was hyperventilating. Finally, she choked out the problem. "Zeke...has been...out cattin' around."

Then came the wailing.

I glanced over my shoulder just in time to catch Daddy looking up from the TV to see where the racket was coming from. He took in all he cared to see and quickly averted his eyes back to MSNBC.

I tried to comfort her. "Now, Tammy Sue, I'm sure that's not true." I was praying to God that it wasn't. Zeke Lyerly's matrimonial escapades were the stuff small town folklore was made of. His first wife had left town, never to be heard from again, after Zeke fired a few rounds of buckshot at her lover. From his vantage point across the street from the Lyerly home, perched high in one of my daddy's live oak trees, Zeke had caught the hapless Casanova creeping out the front door at an hour uncommon for social visits.

Stroking Tammy Sue's back with my free hand, I probed for more information. "What makes you think Zeke has a girlfriend?"

The wails simmered down into sniffles and heaves. "Lately, when I get home in the evenings, he's...*clean*."

I absorbed this for a moment. "Is that unusual?" I asked.

"Well, normally, he gets home just in time for supper, and he still has his work clothes on. Now, as you might imagine, working on cars all day is a grimy business. But for the last two weeks, every day when I get home, he's already had a shower and changed his clothes...and he smells *good*." She dissolved into sobs.

"Maybe he's getting cleaned up for you," I suggested.

"No." She shook her head solemnly. "He's got something on the side, I just know it. A woman can *feel* these things, you understand?"

I took a deep breath, resigned. "So, you want me to follow him and see what he's up to, is that it?"

"Would you, please? I just have to know *for sure*."

I took in the rivulets of mascara running down her cheeks. "Okay," I said. "I'll check it out."

Anxious to get this particular job over and done with, I parked myself across the street from Lyerly's Automotive, in the Edward's Grocery parking lot, at two that afternoon. You might think surveillance is difficult in a green orchid metallic—that's what Ford calls it, but it looks like lime green to me—Ford Escape Hybrid, and normally, you'd be right. But since I flit around this island most days like a butterfly, perching occasionally here and there, folks are used to seeing me out and about. So on the rare occasion when I actually investigate something in town, it's easy enough to hide in plain sight.

I had no sooner settled into stakeout mode—slid low in the seat with the engine off and Jimmy Buffett on, small cooler with Dasani and Cheerwine on the passenger floorboard, camera at the ready, and an open bag of Dove Milk Chocolate Promises handy —when Zeke, whom people often mistake for Blake Shelton—I swear, when he's cleaned up good the resemblance is remarkable —hopped in his Ford F-350 and drove off. I pulled out behind him and smiled and waved as he glanced in the rearview—it would have been rude not to. He waved back and went about his business.

He proceeded down Palmetto Boulevard, around the palm tree-lined park that occupies the town square, and turned down a side street a few blocks beyond the courthouse. I followed him into one of our town's older residential neighborhoods. The cottage-style houses were well maintained, the yards neat. Conveniently, my sister lived a block over, so I had a plausible destination.

Rather abruptly, Zeke turned into Phoebe DiTomei's driveway and pulled into her open garage. Immediately, the automatic door closed behind him. The chicken salad sandwich I'd had for lunch turned sour in my stomach. My imagination failed me in a desperate attempt to invent some innocent explanation as to why Zeke would visit Phoebe at her house in the middle of the afternoon and hide his truck in her garage. Things were looking bleak for Tammy Sue and coiffures all over the island.

Once Southern women grant a Yankee "Nouveau Southern" status, it's an ungodly mess if she proves herself to have been unworthy of such an honor. Adultery committed with a local boy would no doubt qualify as evidence that we native females had been too generous in admitting Phoebe into our sorority, no matter how well she hid the gray. While we might eventually forgive one of our own for such a grievous lapse in manners as sleeping with one of our husbands, the indigenous feminine establishment would never grant clemency to someone who wasn't *from here.*

I drove around the block and pulled into my sister's driveway. She was at work, and I made no pretense of knocking on the door. I slung my Nikon around my neck, walked through her backyard, crossed through two neighboring yards, grateful that they were empty, and climbed over the privacy fence into Phoebe's Garden of Eden.

In addition to being an accomplished hairstylist, Phoebe was an aromatherapist and an avid gardener. Her backyard smelled like a candle shop. Every herb, flower, and tree that had a therapeutic use was growing there. A homemade waterfall in one corner gurgled and sluiced into a small pond where goldfish played. The yard was full of birds happily singing, eating from a collection of feeders, and drinking from the birdbath. Had one sat on my shoulder as I climbed out of the bougainvillea that I landed in, it would have seemed perfectly natural.

I crept up to the back corner of the house and peered into a window. It was a bedroom, decorated in an eclectic style that conjured visions of belly dancers and kidnapped Arabian princesses. No one was currently being ravished within its draped walls. As I moved towards the French doors that stood open to the patio, I heard voices. I froze and listened.

Phoebe's nasal tones wafted through the doors. "You want the usual, or are we getting kinky today?"

I'd been a guest in her home a few times and knew that these doors opened into her living room. It seemed an odd setting for getting kinky in broad daylight, but hey, I'm pretty much a champagne, candlelight, and soft music kind of girl myself. What do I know about kinky?

"You know how I like it, that's why I come here."

I wasn't expecting romance—it's just not in Zeke's nature. But his tone was so matter-of-fact it made me scrunch up my face in that expression that Mamma has warned me thousands of times is going to give me early wrinkles.

I dropped to my belly. Carefully gripping my camera in my hands, I used my elbows and hipbones to propel myself across the patio. I raised my camera and scanned the living room for my subjects, sending up a silent prayer that they still had their clothes on. Finding my targets, I brought them into focus.

Convulsions of stifled belly laughter racked my body, making it difficult to hold on to the camera. I caught them *flagrante delicto*, all right. Just as they were preparing for a clandestine haircut. I took a picture; I'm not sure why—maybe it was the sheer incongruity of Zeke with the pink drape over his work clothes—

then slithered back across the patio and sat down to mull the situation over.

Luther Baynard was the town's only barber and he was within shouting distance of seventy years old. He was a cantankerous but beloved old coot who had cut the hair of virtually every man on the island from the first time their mommas had brought them into his shop with tears and cameras. A fashion slave Luther was not. He cut hair the same way he always had—short—regardless of what the client asked for. Zeke wore his curly brown locks a couple of inches past his collar. Luther had obviously not taken scissors to his head.

But for a guy like Zeke, sitting in the beauty shop amidst matrons in curlers and soccer moms in foils would not be an option. Phoebe had obviously been prevailed upon to give him private haircuts. I sat there long enough to verify that a trim was the only service he'd come for, then slipped back to my car the same way I came.

From there I followed Zeke straight home. It was still early, not even three o'clock, and I had planned to wait around and see if he came back out, but Daddy called me on my cell phone. He'd gotten another computer virus—this one was displaying random pictures of naked men and he couldn't make it stop—and he needed me back over at the flea market ASAP.

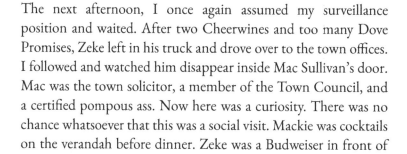

The next afternoon, I once again assumed my surveillance position and waited. After two Cheerwines and too many Dove Promises, Zeke left in his truck and drove over to the town offices. I followed and watched him disappear inside Mac Sullivan's door. Mac was the town solicitor, a member of the Town Council, and a certified pompous ass. Now here was a curiosity. There was no chance whatsoever that this was a social visit. Mackie was cocktails on the verandah before dinner. Zeke was a Budweiser in front of the TV with supper.

I didn't have long to wait. Zeke was headed back to the truck inside of five minutes. From there, he drove straight to the brick ranch he shared with Tammy Sue across the street from the house I grew up in. I thought I had hit another dead end. It was three forty-five, and he was home alone. Since Tammy usually didn't leave the flea market until five thirty, I decided to stick around just in case he left again. Hoping Daddy wouldn't have another pornography-related emergency that demanded my attention, I pulled into my parents' driveway and slid down in my seat, watching the Lyerly door through my driver's side mirror.

Ten minutes later, Zeke came back out of the house, sporting full military camouflage attire. He stole a couple of furtive glances around and then climbed back into his truck and peeled out.

I followed him out Marsh Point Drive, to the northwest side of the island. One thing was clear, unless he was having an affair with an outdoorsy sort who favored daytime romps in the sweet-grass—a type of woman in short supply in our town—he wasn't meeting a girlfriend. He pulled down an old dirt road that led back to nothing but forty acres of woods and a freshwater lagoon that backed up to the salt marsh. I knew that the road dead-ended about a mile down, so just before the last curve, I pulled over and got out for a stroll through the woods. I slipped my Sig Sauer 9 out of my Kate Spade bag, tucked it into the back of my capris, and made a mental note to charge Tammy Sue extra for this.

I waded through the dense, exotic vegetation that grows between the pine trees and live oaks, watching carefully for snakes. I purely hate snakes. After about ten minutes, I heard someone tromping through the woods ahead of me. I made my way towards the noise, darting behind trees for cover.

According to the legend of Zeke Lyerly, as told by Zeke Lyerly, he was once an Army Ranger and had spent years fighting the drug lords in the South American jungles for the DEA. His stories were the kind that his buddies pretended to believe while consuming mass quantities of alcohol, but no one in town took seriously. The only verifiable facts were that he had been in the

Army and he had spent twenty years away from home. If there were any truth to his tales—a possibility I had never before entertained—he would surely pick up on the fact that I was trailing him through the woods.

Suddenly, he was right in front of me. I crouched behind a big oak and watched him for a moment. In his hand, he held a pistol with a silencer attached. He was creeping through the woods, obviously stalking someone. About this time, I started to question the wisdom of following Zeke Lyerly into the woods. I retrieved my friend Sig from the small of my back.

Zeke assumed a firing stance—feet wide, arms locked forward —and took aim. He was standing directly between me and his target, so I couldn't see the victim.

I cringed as I heard the *pfft-pfft* sound of the gun being fired.

"Gotcha, you sonavabitch!" he muttered.

I watched wide-eyed as he stuck the pistol in the back of his pants, strode through the trees, and reached down to grab his prey. He was dragging something dead as he backed up. As he passed not ten feet in front of me, I saw what it was.

It was a large pink hog.

I watched him drag that hog all the way over to the edge of the lagoon, where he dropped it by the water. Then he backed up a few strides, sat down on the bank, and lit a cigarette. He just sat there, smoking and staring at the water, as if he was waiting on something. After a few moments, I noticed what looked like a log drifting in the lagoon toward the shoreline. Then, the log had eyes. In horror, I watched as an alligator that must have been fourteen feet long opened its great mouth and snatched up that hog. Zeke just sat there calmly smoking his Camel.

The alligator retreated with its dinner, and I walked up and collapsed beside Zeke. He didn't even look up. It was as if he'd known I was there the whole time.

"Zeke." I greeted him as casually as if I'd passed him on the street.

"Liz." He nodded.

"What in the name of common sense are you doing?" I asked him straight up.

"What does it look like I'm doing?" he retorted.

I thought that over for a minute. "Well, it *looks like* you're assassinating hogs and feeding them to an alligator...which I'm pretty sure no one else knows resides in that lagoon."

"Oh, there's a whole family of them," he said easily. "Nobody ever comes out here except high school kids, and they're too preoccupied with discovering sex to pay much attention to what's in the water—it's too murky for skinny dipping."

"So why are you feeding the hogs to them?"

"This is a covert operation," he informed me. "I'll need your word that you won't compromise it, or else I may have to feed *you* to the alligators." He grinned amiably, as if to let me know that he was just kidding about that last part, but I wasn't a hundred percent sure. He was still staring at the water.

"Okay, my lips are sealed."

He nodded. "A small group of concerned citizens—Mackie, your daddy, and our mayor—is paying me to transport the hogs to the hereafter. I use a silencer so no one will hear the gunshots. I feed the hogs to the alligators to get rid of the evidence, and because it's easier than burying them or hauling them off. The idea is for folks to think they're dying out of natural causes."

For the first time since I had sat down, he looked straight at me. "Now what are *you* doing here?" There was a hard edge to his voice that I'd never heard before, one that seemed unaccountably at home on his tongue. I suddenly realized that I was sitting beside a stranger. I felt more mystified than threatened.

Dark currents roiled in intelligent blue eyes. There was a worldly awareness, layers of a person I had never suspected lived inside this personification of a Southern cliché. In retrospect, I think it must have been that while he was stalking those hogs, he flashed back to another place and time. He was doing familiar things, tracking his prey through the dense forest, and in the act, he had inadvertently slipped out of character, just for a moment.

It was a revelation. Only later would I realize how brilliant Zeke Lyerly's disguise was: he hid his genuine self, at least a large part of him, behind the truth. In telling us his colorful, larger-than-life adventures all these years, he had deliberately created the persona of a slightly nutty but loveable, harmless good ole boy that told unbelievable but entertaining stories.

A long moment went by as I considered how to answer his question. Client confidentiality is important to me, but in this case, it seemed like the best thing was to simply tell him the truth. "Your wife thinks you're having an affair."

"*What?*" He screwed up his face in disbelief, mask safely back in place. "Why in the hell would she think that?"

"Apparently because you're clean when she gets home these days."

"Ahhh." His face lit with understanding.

"What am I supposed to tell her?"

"Well, you can't tell her the truth. First, she'd be mad as hell. She does not want these hogs hurt. Second, she never could keep a secret, and if this gets out, Mackie will have a seizure, and he won't pay me, either."

We both sat there for a minute, staring across the water.

Then, I had an idea. "What if I tell her the truth, up to a point? I'll tell her I followed you home, and you got there at three forty-five. Then, it will be up to you to convince her that you're all clean and sweet smelling for *some reason* other than you've been dragging dead hogs around and needed to wash the stench off." I batted my eyelashes flirtatiously at him to drive home my point.

He grinned. "Sounds like a plan."

"I won't take any money from her." I stood and brushed myself off. Still unsettled, I was eager to leave that isolated corner of the island with its wild hogs, alligators, and faux-redneck Rambo.

"I'll pay you for your time," he offered.

"No, thanks," I said. "I'll write it off as research."

"Huh?"

"I'm writing a book on the eccentricities of the Southern Male."

"Don't use my name," he warned, some of the earlier edge creeping back into his voice.

"Oh, don't worry," I assured him. "All the names have been changed to protect the wives and mothers."

Highlights & Hot Lead

Shannelle Johnson breezed into Phoebe DiTomei's Day Spa with her customary grace. Blow-dryers clicked off and a dozen wagging tongues tripped and flopped wordlessly, like flounder on a pier. What commanded our attention wasn't so much the petite ash blonde as the shotgun she carried, a curious accessory to her crisp, white linen pantsuit.

Clack-snap. She chambered a shell and aimed at the ceiling. "Which one of you lying hussies is trying to snare my Jared with someone else's bastard?"

No one stepped forward.

Phoebe's was slam full that morning, just hours before the Stella Maris senior prom. Grace Sullivan and I were the only clients with high school diplomas. Half a dozen varsity cheerleaders rotated between the hair, nail, and make-up stations.

Phoebe had my blonde highlights half foiled. "Liz," she hissed through clenched teeth, "do something!"

My brother Blake is the police chief in our small Southern town, and I guess she presumed it was my responsibility by association. Or perhaps she thought because I was a private investigator by trade, I had related credentials. Flattered as I was by her confidence, I entertained no illusions I was equipped to deal with a deranged, shotgun-toting judge's wife.

Across the room, Grace Sullivan appeared insanely calm in her pink drape and curlers. "Shannelle...Honey, are you off your hormones again?"

"As a matter of fact, I am." Shannelle cast her friend an irritated glare. "You know I hate taking pills. But that's irrelevant."

Phoebe spoke in soothing tones: "You look a little tense. How about we get you in for an aromatherapy massage?"

"I do not *need* a massage." Shannelle narrowed her eyes and beamed a round of poison darts in every direction. Then she advanced.

We all sucked in lungfuls of color fumes, polish remover, and jasmine scented candles.

Shannelle glided over to Kelsey Elliott, the cheerleader closest to the door.

Kelsey quivered, but held her fingers splayed wide, so as not to muss her manicure.

"I understand Jared's escorting you to the prom, Kelsey." Shannelle paced in front of the nail station.

"Yes, Ma'am."

"This your first date with Jared?"

"Yes, Ma'am. We're just friends, really..."

Shannelle eyed Kelsey suspiciously and moved on to the pedicure chair, where Reese Beauthorpe sat with cotton between her half-pink toes.

"Reese?" Shannelle raised an eyebrow.

"Yes, ma'am?" Reese whispered.

"You still dating Michael Simmons?"

"Yes, ma'am."

"Steady?"

"Yes, ma'am...for two years now."

"That's what I thought." Shannelle spun to her right and spied Emma Waters. The judge's wife drew herself up to her full five feet.

Emma dropped from the makeup chair to her knees and commenced praying The Lord's Prayer, eyes squeezed shut.

"Emma!" Shannelle snapped.

Emma stopped praying, opened one eye, and looked up fearfully.

"You and Jared went out last weekend, didn't you? To a party?"

"Well..." stammered Emma. "It was a church party."

Shannelle leaned down. "What did you do afterwards?"

"Shannelle!" Grace was losing patience. "For Heaven's sake. Put down that gun and let's get you some tea and a Valium."

"Hush up, Grace!" Shannelle glared over her shoulder, then turned back to Emma. They were nose to nose.

"We went for a drive," Emma sobbed.

Shannelle's voice was low and dangerous. "Where did you stop?"

"Nowhere. Honest, Mrs. Johnson. We drove around and talked a while, then Jared took me home. I have to be in by midnight."

"How many times have you been out with my son?"

Emma clamped her eyes shut. "Three."

Shannelle backed off. She seemed to be considering Emma's response. "Who else has he been out with?"

"I don't think anybody. He's real busy with baseball."

Like a rodeo clown, I jumped into the ring to distract the bull. "Shannelle, I have an idea."

She swung towards me, then sashayed in my direction, a speculative look on her patrician face. I wondered if she was recalling the stories in the news about teenage boys and the older women having their babies.

Shannelle stopped in front of the hydraulic chair where I sat with my half-highlighted hair. "Elizabeth?"

Over her shoulder, I glimpsed Elvis Glendawn peering saucer-eyed through cupped hands in the window. Elvis was my age—thirty—but developmentally challenged. He spent his days patrolling the town on his bicycle, helping Blake maintain law and order. Surely he would run and get him lickety-split.

"Elizabeth!" Shannelle snapped me to attention.

"I was thinking Grace could tell you if anyone here is in the family way." Grace was our town psychic. Ever since she nearly drowned in the ocean when she was seventeen, she'd been blessed with special talents. I was reasonably certain that Shannelle's bastard grandchild was a figment of her hormone-imbalanced imagination, and if not, well, at least this exercise would keep us all alive till the cavalry arrived.

Grace—my Godmother, the woman who had spoiled me with spectacular flair my entire life—glowered at me like she wished she'd fed me to the alligators as an infant.

Shannelle's eyes sparked. "Of course, she can. Emma! Get yourself over here and let Grace lay hands on you."

Emma pulled herself up and bolted right on over to Grace. She was too eager to be guilty.

Grace muled up. "This is outrageous. Shannelle Johnson, I—"

"If she's innocent, she's got nothing to worry about," said Shannelle.

Grace pursed her lips together, studied the ceiling for a moment, then motioned Emma closer.

Emma complied.

Grace reached up, gently laid both hands on Emma's washboard stomach, and closed her eyes. You could have heard the ferns grow in that salon.

"Well?" Shannelle tapped her Stuart Weitzman sandal.

"This child is no more expecting a baby than you are, you lunatic," Grace informed her.

Surprise flickered across Shannelle's face. She pivoted, raised her chin, and issued a summons to the shampoo station. "Jessica Ravenel. You're next."

Jessica scooted across the room.

Grace flashed Shannelle another mean look. "Exactly what

makes you believe that any of these girls is about to make you a grandmother?"

"If you must know, I overheard Jared tell Ansley he was going to be a father, and that the mother of his child was one of the senior cheerleaders. I don't think he'd concoct that particular lie to tell his sister, do you?"

Grace paled. "I suppose not. But—"

"Just tell me if it's Jessica," Shannelle spat.

"And what if it is?" Grace demanded. "You going to shoot her right here in the beauty parlor?"

"Excuse me, Mrs. Johnson?" Emma the Innocent raised her hand.

"What is it?"

"Ma'am, if you please, exactly what did Jared say?"

"I just told you," Shannelle snapped.

"You see, we're doing this project in Sociology—"

"Emma, do you fail to grasp the seriousness of this situation? This is scarcely the time to prattle on about your school work," said Shannelle.

Kelsey stared at Emma. "But that's just it, Mrs. Johnson."

Shannelle swiveled her head in Kelsey's direction. I swear, it looked like it spun all the way around. "What's just it?"

"We're studying family planning," Kelsey explained.

"I'd say that unit came a little too late, wouldn't you?" Shannelle was unenlightened, but Reese's eyes widened with understanding.

"Mrs. Grayson paired us up—we had pretend weddings and everything," Reese said. "For a month, we have to carry around an egg in a basket—like it's a real baby. One of the parents has to take care of it constantly."

"You expect me to believe that this project is what Jared was referring to?" Shannelle scrunched her face up in a way she never would've had she been herself—that much expression was likely to cause wrinkles.

"Yes, ma'am...that must be it. I mean Jared...he's too preoccupied with baseball to have a serious girlfriend." Emma looked relieved and sad at the same time. "I'm his make-believe wife."

Shannelle pondered this information. "That *would* explain his complete lack of concern."

She lowered the shotgun and looked at Phoebe. "Do you have time to touch up my roots?" And just like that, she propped that shotgun in the corner, sat down beside Grace, and picked up the latest Southern Living.

The door chimed as Blake and Elvis charged in. Blake stopped short and took in the apparent normalcy. "Everything all right in here?"

Grace smiled at him sweetly. "Why, of course, Darlin', why wouldn't it be?"

Blake glanced at Elvis, then his eyes found mine. "Liz?"

I gave him my best, what's the matter with you look. "Everything's fine."

I perceived he couldn't make up his mind whether Elvis had overreacted to something he thought he saw—which occasionally happened—or we were hiding something, a more likely circumstance.

Blake's eyes scanned the room. "Phoebe," he asked, "that your shotgun?"

"Heavens no, Blake, that's mine," Shannelle said, not glancing up from her magazine.

"Is there something here that needs shooting, Mrs. Johnson?" Blake asked.

"Blake Talbot! Have you taken leave of your senses? This is a beauty shop," said Shannelle.

"Exactly. What is it doing here?" He strode over and stared down at the gun in question.

"Right now it's just sitting there against the wall. After Phoebe freshens my hairstyle, I'm going to carry it over to the hardware store so Walt Stevens can take a look at it. I went to shoot a squirrel yesterday and it misfired." Shannelle turned the page. That issue of Southern Living positively enthralled her.

Blake scrutinized her for a Savannah moment. He turned to Phoebe. "You're sure everything's all right?"

For three seconds, we all held our breath. We liked Phoebe, but she was, after all, a Yankee. Her loyalty was not a matter of ancestral obligation.

"Everything's fine." Phoebe smiled.

Blake confiscated the gun. "Mrs. Johnson, I'm heading over to the hardware store myself. Why don't I drop this off for you? Save you the trouble."

My brother was no fool. He wouldn't wrangle with a judge's wife unnecessarily, but he wouldn't leave a notorious nut in possession of a firearm either.

"Why, Blake, aren't you the sweetest thing?" Shannelle oozed.

"Happy to help."

He sent me one last, I know you're up to something look. "Ladies." He nodded and was out the door, Elvis in tow.

A few seconds passed and no one spoke.

Shannelle looked up from her magazine. "All beauty treatments are on me today, girls. How would that be?"

"In that case, I'm having a massage and a mud bath," Grace declared.

Emma's eyes lit up. "A massage!"

"Why yes, we'll all have one!" Shannelle declared. "Phoebe, don't you have some mimosas around here somewhere? We'll just keep our little misunderstanding between us girls."

Everything Is Relative

"Do you think we'll have enough food?" Mamma dried her hands on a dishtowel. Her worried eyes searched mine.

I shut the refrigerator and leaned against the door until it relented. Something shifted inside. Praying nothing had fallen into her pumpkin cake, I stared at her. She asked me this same question before every holiday, birthday, and funeral spread.

"Mamma." I plopped onto a French Provincial counter stool. "We have two Whirlpool side-by-sides slam full of food. Every flat surface in this house has something to eat on it."

"I bet it won't be any good." She spooned a bite of squash casserole from the mixing bowl. "Taste this."

I opened my mouth to protest and she stuck the spoon in. I closed my eyes and savored the perfect marriage of vegetable and artery-clogging sauce. She knew it was delicious. Her recipe, one she called "Mother's Day Squash Casserole," because she invented it one year for a Mother's Day picnic, had won both a Southern Living contest and first place in the church cookbook. I groaned. "Please don't feed me anything else."

I generally consider myself a sane person. But every year, sometime between Halloween and New Year's Day, I ponder the possibility I may be mistaken. I'm either the only sane one in the bunch, or I, Liz Talbot, am as nutty as Aunt Regina's Festive Holiday Congealed Delight. That year, my annual self-analysis began the day before Thanksgiving.

"You don't like it." Mamma gave me her wounded look.

"Oh puh-leeze." I rolled my eyes. "Is Ray Kennedy coming?"

"Where else would he spend Thanksgiving?"

Mamma throws an annual Thanksgiving circus for our family —both her side and my daddy's. In addition to this cast of certifiable lunatics, over the years she's added friends and neighbors to the guest list: Humphrey Pearson, the town nudist, who had a falling out with his own family regarding the definition of dressing for dinner—he and Mamma compromised on a loin cloth and mesh tank top; the neighbors across the street, Zeke and Tammy Sue Lyerly, whose family migrated elsewhere and haven't kept in touch—that's a whole nother saga; and Ray Kennedy— no relation—a guy I feel genuinely sorry for, but can barely tolerate.

Orphans from some European country I can't pronounce, Ray and his sister were adopted by religious zealots in Pennsylvania forty years ago. I'm not sure what happened to the sister, but he hasn't seen her in years. Ray hasn't lived a happy life, is what I'm saying. He and my daddy crossed paths when I was ten. Ray was trying to sell Daddy some damn thing. From the trunk of his car, he peddled bee pollen, aura spray, ear candles, protective helmets guaranteed to prevent the government and clairvoyant aliens from reading your mind, and so forth. Daddy brought him home for supper one night and Mamma fed him. He's been hanging around ever since. I try—honestly, I do—to be nice to him. What kind of person is rude to a European orphan? But he annoys me.

When I was sixteen, he showed up in his rusted-out dinosaur of a diesel Oldsmobile, ten minutes before my first date with Jackson Beauthorpe, and parked smack in front of the house. When Jackson arrived, Ray commenced his pitch for a new colon cleansing system. I know, I'm thirty-one years old and should have gotten over the humiliation a long time ago, but trust me, that is but one example in hundreds of things he's done to challenge my sunny disposition.

Mamma poured the squash into a casserole dish and sprinkled butter-crumb topping over it. "Would you put this in the refrigerator in the garage?"

"Nothing else will fit."

"Just squeeze it in."

Thanksgiving draws a crowd of thirty, give or take, at Mamma and Daddy's house on Stella Maris—that's the island near Charleston where we live. There used to be more of us, but through the years, the gala has suffered attrition. My sister, Merry, started taking vacations over Thanksgiving three years ago. Somehow, that's the only time she can get away.

The State of South Carolina incarcerated my aunt Angelina following an unfortunate domestic incident in which circumstances compelled her to shoot her brother-in-law's ear off—their affair ended badly—so she can't make it either. Aunt Angelina is married to Mamma's brother Wade. The brother-in-law who lost the ear was on the other side of her family. We don't know much about him. These folks aren't blood relations, is what I'm saying.

And then there's Mamma's youngest brother, Cecil, who took a Greyhound to Florida a few years back. The last we heard he'd started his own church somewhere near Orlando. He sent Mamma a postcard once with a picture of him, shaved bald, cloaked in a white robe, standing in front of a statue of Mary that wept blood. He had an albino boa constrictor draped across his shoulders as big around as a cat. I guess no one told Cecil that the snakes handled in religious services were generally the poisonous kind. We don't talk about him. It upsets Mamma.

Don't get me started on my cousin, Marci the Schemer.

I wilted as I carried that squash into the garage. I'd arrived at nine a.m. to help Mamma cook and decorate. Since she insisted all thirty of us sit down together—at the same table—this was more involved than throwing on a tablecloth and getting out the china.

Even with the leaves, her antique mahogany Duncan Phyfe wouldn't seat thirty, so we slid eight banquet tables together on the screened porch to create one monstrosity of a feasting plateau. We disguised the utilitarian tables with ivory floor-length cloths and a thirty-foot sage-colored runner Mamma had custom made. A cornucopia, brimming with vibrant vegetables and fruits, graced the center, and we strung garlands of fall leaves on top of the runner. Twelve hurricane lanterns with fat candles would provide the lighting. Mamma loves what candlelight does for the complexion.

I glanced at the clock as I drug myself back into the kitchen. "Mamma, it's ten thirty, and we've run out of places to put food."

"Go on home and get some rest. I'll see you in the morning." She patted my arm.

"You're turning in, too, right?"

"In a minute." She fixated on scouring the sink.

I knew better. As soon as I was out the door she'd decide she needed one more dessert because she didn't have anything lemon, or set to cleaning something that had already been cleaned three times. I walked into the den where Daddy had nodded off an hour before watching that man who screams about investments and all such as that on CNN. "Daddy." I shook him gently.

"Huh?" He startled awake. "Stocks are in the toilet."

"Wake up and make Mamma go to bed. I'm going home." I hugged his neck.

He climbed out of the leather chair. "Cousin Madam, come turn down the bed so I can get in."

Although I come from a long line of basket cases, despite Daddy's habit of calling Mamma "Cousin Madam," we are not, so far as I know, inbred.

Showtime was six p.m. At five forty-five, Michael—oh boy, how to explain Michael? For starters, he's my cousin Marci's ex-husband. He and I were college sweethearts before she snookered him away from me. He's been my brother, Blake's, best friend since they were toddlers, and Michael's been trying to get me to marry him since spring, but it's complicated. I pined for that man for years while he was married to Marci the Schemer, but just now, I'm partial to my partner, Nate. Okay, Nate is also my ex-husband's brother. I told you, it's complicated. Mamma invited Michael.

Anyway, Michael, me, Mamma and Daddy, and Blake were enjoying a pre-chaos glass of Beaujolais in the family room. I should have drunk more and faster. I brought the glass to my lips for maybe my third sip when a car door slammed.

Blake looked out the window. "The teetotalers are here," he announced.

Mamma hopped up and snatched that wine glass right out of my hand. Lickety-split, she gathered everyone else's and scurried toward the kitchen.

"Oh, Mamma, for crying out loud," I complained.

Grandmamma Moore referred to alcohol as Devil Juice. Aunt Regina and Uncle Aaron were of the same mind. The best you could hope for if you imbibed in their presence was a frigid cloud of sanctimony. Worst-case scenario, they'd quote scripture at us and leave. So, Mamma insisted we hide the booze anytime they made the trip from Summerville, which wasn't often.

Don't get me wrong: *none* of us are alcoholics. Well, except Daddy's cousin, Ponder, and he's been doing real good since that last visit to rehab. And, well, all right, Ponder's half-sister, Miller, is a lush, and there's no getting around that. But most of us are moderate drinkers. We like wine with dinner and an occasional drink of liquor. If ever there was an occasion that called for hard liquor, it was a Talbot/Moore family gathering. For years, we didn't even get to have a glass of wine before the teetotalers arrived —Mamma was afraid they'd smell it on our breath. Lately, she's relaxed the rules, perhaps in need of fortification.

The abstainers joined us in the family room, followed by my

cousin Isaac, Aunt Regina and Uncle Aaron's youngest boy. Now, I would be willing to wager a year's supply of Estée Lauder that Isaac does not share his parents' aversion to alcohol. If I had to guess, I'd say Devil Juice was one of his tamer indulgences. It's just a guess.

Everyone hugged everybody else—except Uncle Aaron, he's afraid of germs—and we all settled back into the over-stuffed family room furniture.

"There's iced tea and coffee in the kitchen. Can I get anybody anything?" Mamma asked.

Blake and I looked at her, thinking about the Beaujolais that just went down the sink, but neither of us said a word.

"No, thank you. I'll wait," said Grandmamma Moore, as if sweet tea was an indulgence she'd save till later.

Isaac sat by Michael and me on the sofa. "What's it been?"

I tried not to stare at his spiked turquoise hair, the studded dog collar around his neck, or the ring in his nose. It wasn't a big ring, maybe the size of a dime, and it matched the stud in his left eyebrow, to which it was attached by a delicate chain. The hair had been magenta the last time I'd seen him. "I'm afraid I've lost track. It's been a while. How're things with you?" It was difficult to carry on a conversation with someone whose looks were that much of a distraction.

"Same ole same ole."

I had to wonder what that meant for him. "How's work?" Isaac worked for The Department of Homeland Security, a fact that had caused me to stare at the ceiling a night or two, unable to sleep.

"If I told you, I'd have to kill you." His laugh was this god-awful honking sound.

Michael jolted. The honking always startled him.

"Hey, y'all." Mamma's brother, Wade, came through the front door, followed by her other brother, Earl.

Isaac swaggered into the kitchen to get some iced tea, and

Wade took his place on the sofa. "Hey, I got a joke for you," he said.

Because Wade's jokes were nearly always tasteless—and never funny—I flashed him what must have been a discouraging look.

"Don't you want to hear it?" Wade shifted gears. "Did you hear they're making kids learn Mandarin Chinese in schools now? It's part of the Chinese takeover. We're handing the U.S. of A. over to the Chinese. You'll see."

Michael and I looked at each other. Every year, Wade's sanity circled further down the drain. We didn't know how to respond without sending him into a full-blown rant.

Thankfully, Mamma returned from the kitchen. "Now, Wade, you know we don't talk politics before dinner." She smiled, but there was steel in her eyes. "Or during, or after."

"Alls I'm saying is y'all better be ready," he said.

"Are you planning to move on out to Montana and stockpile some weapons?" I asked.

He fixed a cold glare on me and drew his head back like a snake coiling to strike. "Why?"

I was kidding. But in that moment, I knew the thought had crossed his mind.

Michael stood and pulled me to my feet. "Let's get some tea."

We hastened into Mamma's Southern Living showcase-home kitchen—commercial-grade appliances, granite countertops, old-world-style cabinets that looked like furniture. You get the picture. Daddy and Uncle Earl stood next to the fireplace. Against direct orders, they were discussing politics or something like it.

I went to the sink to wash my hands.

"It's these conglomerates," Uncle Earl said. "They're deliberately trying to collapse our economy, so we can be merged with Mexico and Canada, that's what's behind these gas prices."

Daddy gave him the knitted-brow-no-eye-contact nod. I knew he didn't buy into Uncle Earl's theories, but, always the gracious host, Daddy wouldn't contradict the crackpot to his face.

"Hey there!" Daddy's cousin Miller made her entrance into

the kitchen, tossing her signature long, layered mane of bright red hair. Among other murky business activities about which it was best not to be too informed, Miller was in real estate. Her big-toothed grin adorned several local billboards.

"Hey, Miller, how are you?" I asked.

"Oh, I'm great, just great." She smiled so wide the corners of her mouth nearly touched her ears. Her eyes had a glazed-over look, as they nearly always did. Odds were she'd started drinking early in the day.

"What's the latest on the subdivision?" Michael asked, in reference to a piece of property in Charleston that Miller planned to develop. Michael was in residential construction, and they had discussed him building some of the houses, something he'd never, ever actually do, but it gave us something to talk about.

"Just a few details to take care of. I'm going to Belize next week. Soon as I get back, we'll talk." Miller slapped Michael on the back and ducked into the family room.

Daddy's eyes met mine across the room. He shook his head.

Uncle Earl stepped out into the screened porch. As the door closed behind him, I moved closer to Daddy and Michael followed.

"I can't believe Miller's still running around loose," I said.

Daddy shrugged. "She sold her house and put an Airstream trailer behind her daddy's. Got a mailbox in front of it and everything."

"That's where she's living?" asked Michael. "What about Arlo and the twins?"

"They're still living in the house," Daddy said.

"I thought you said she sold it." I was confused.

"Well, she sold it to some friends of hers in Belize, and they're renting it back to Arlo."

"Oh, my stars. How much does Miller owe the IRS?" I asked.

"One point five million is what she told me they want. But she doesn't think she's going to have to pay it."

47

"What would make her think that?" Michael asked, wide-eyed.

Daddy sighed. "Something about she's not a U.S. citizen, so she doesn't owe any taxes. She hasn't filed a return in fifteen years."

"What?" I felt my jaw drop and my eyes pop clear out of my head like one of those cartoon characters. I could have sworn I heard an abandon ship horn.

"She says she's renounced her citizenship," Daddy said.

"Oh, please." I had this image of Miller standing in the town square shouting, "I renounce thee, I renounce thee, I renounce thee."

"What about the property in West Ashley?" Michael asked. This was the tract where the subdivision was supposed to go up.

"She sold that to the folks in Belize, too. Says she's going to develop it for them. But now they're afraid the IRS might seize it."

"I'd say that's a valid fear." I nodded.

The noise level in the family room had picked up, and groups milled around outside.

Mamma came into the kitchen, followed by Ray Kennedy. "Everyone's here," she said.

"R.C. Bird!" Daddy greeted Ray with a slap on the shoulder. R.C. Bird was the name Daddy hung on Ray years ago, for reasons unknown, but that's what most of us called him anymore.

"Hey, how's it going?" R.C. glanced around the room, eyes bright with excitement.

We all said hey and all that.

"Liz, honey, help me get the food in the chafing dishes. Michael, tell everyone to get drinks. Frank, it's time to carve the turkey." Mamma moved toward the carving board. She'd let Daddy do the cutting, under supervision.

I went to the sink to wash my hands.

Everyone was cruising through the kitchen, getting drinks, and wandering outside. The soundtrack played the usual cacophony of large family meals: the chatter of seven different conversations, ice falling into glasses, the clink of serving utensils, the thud of things being dropped, the shotgun blast from the backyard.

"Frank, I told you to lock that gun cabinet." Mamma's eyes accused Daddy.

Everyone but the three of us pressed their noses to the windows to see what was getting shot.

"I did, Carolyn," he said. "Zeke brought his own. It's new...he just wanted to show it around."

"It doesn't sound like he's showing it around," she said through gritted teeth.

"Well, I told him about that bobcat that's been getting the rabbits. He said he'd keep an eye out. Maybe he's spotted him," Daddy speculated.

"In the dark?" Mamma snapped.

She strode over to the door, jerked it open, and stuck her head out. "Zeke, please put the shotgun away. It's Thanksgiving. Y'all come on in, it's time to eat."

Michael came up behind me at the sink as I was rinsing my hands and put his arms around me. "That water must be 200 degrees. Your hands are scalded," he said.

I turned the water off and dried my hands. "I'm handling food," I told him.

This I know: You won't find a more sumptuous Thanksgiving spread than the one in my mamma's kitchen. We had turkey and gravy and two kinds of dressing—cornbread style and oyster—ham, mashed potato casserole, sweet potato soufflé, corn pie, asparagus with hollandaise, squash casserole, old-fashioned green beans, tomato pie, layered salad, broccoli casserole, cranberry sauce, and Aunt Regina's Festive Holiday Congealed Delight. And yeast rolls. Pumpkin pie, pumpkin cake, maplewalnut cheesecake, Mamma's famous chocolate cake, and a punch bowl of trifle. The aromas merged into a heady fragrance that could be named Home For the Holidays or All I Want for Christmas is My Arteries Scraped.

"All right, everybody, it's time to say the blessing," Mamma said.

All thirty of us crammed into the kitchen. Before holiday meals, we sing the doxology as a blessing. It's our tradition. We used to hold hands, back before Uncle Aaron became afraid of germs and Mamma invited Humphrey. A few of my uncles refuse to hold hands with a man in a loin cloth, regardless of the circumstances. Blake—one of the few who can sing—started us off by singing the last line. "Praise Father, Son, and Holy Ghost."

While we were singing, I looked around the room. Everyone was smiling. We all drooled in anticipation of the feast, and although no one had any idea why, being together on holidays caused a feeling of peace to come over us. But the happiest face in the room—and the loudest off-key voice—was R.C. Bird: he beamed and belted out every note.

Then, Mamma offered a short prayer. "Father in Heaven, we thank you for these many blessings you have bestowed upon us. Bless this food to our use, and us to thy service. Bless our children, and..."

Okay, it wasn't that short. Anytime Mamma gets us all in the same room with God, she makes good use of the time. Next came the part where everyone tries to get someone else to go first in line. Blake had little patience with this curious custom, so he grabbed a plate and got things started. R.C. Bird followed closely behind, and everyone fell in.

I stepped over to the sink to wash my hands. Michael came up behind me and touched the small of my back. "Sweetheart, you just washed your hands."

"But we're getting ready to eat." I flashed him a smile that said, Silly, of course, we wash our hands before we eat.

He just shook his head.

We piled our plates high and found our places at the table. Michael and I sat near the end, across from Blake and R.C. Bird.

As we engaged in the standard dinner table small talk...oohing and ahhing over the food, and so forth, it struck me again how happy R.C. looked.

"Regina," he called down the table. "Excellent Jell-O." He gave her a big thumbs-up.

Now, Aunt Regina is very proud of her Festive Holiday Congealed Delight. She does not appreciate it being referred to as Jell-O. She smiled that little thin smile of hers. "Thank you so very much, Ray."

R.C. went back to eating. After a few minutes, he said to Mamma, "Carolyn, this turkey is much better than last year's."

Mamma just raised her eyebrows, smiled, and nodded. She'd prepared the twenty-two-pound turkey whose bones we were gnawing the same way she's been doing it for thirty years, and not one of those birds had ever been anything less than succulent.

"And I particularly like that oyster dressing," R.C. continued.

"Liz made the oyster dressing," Blake said.

"She's coming right along, isn't she?" R.C. nudged Blake.

"Liz has always been a good cook." Blake, like any good brother, wanted to make sure I didn't feel slighted by the left-handed compliment.

"She's following in the family tradition."

"Thank you, R.C., I'm glad you're enjoying it," I said.

He was trying real hard to let everyone know how much he appreciated the food and so forth, but, bless his heart, it just kept coming out wrong.

Daddy came to his rescue, complimenting R.C. on how good the outdoor lights looked. Every year, Daddy cons R.C. into putting up a million little white lights on trees, shrubs, along a section of fence—wherever Mamma wants them.

R.C. glowed. "They do look good, don't they? Took me all day last Saturday to get 'em up, but it was worth it, don't you think?" He grinned at me.

"They look real festive," I said. He was so happy to have a part in the family holiday traditions that he didn't mind a single bit that it involved a rickety extension ladder, sticker bushes, and probable electric shock. Blake sure had pitched a fit every time he'd had to do it.

"We've got the best display on the island," R.C. said.

I was taken aback by that remark, not because the lights weren't beautiful—they were—but because of the way he included himself in the family. Like I said, R.C. had been coming around for years, but he wasn't family.

Then I looked around the table at that crazy quilt of characters—my security blanket. People who were there when I had my first dance recital, when I graduated from college, and when I'd had a close encounter with a sociopath who nearly killed me four years ago. Through sickness, health, scandals, and family brawls, they were there. I belonged to them—God help me—and they to me.

It became clear to me that fall evening in the house where I grew up, with a feast worthy of kings on the table, surrounded by arguably the largest gathering of free-range loonies in any one place in the galaxy, that the connectedness we shared was something I had long taken for granted—and R.C. Bird desperately craved.

I smiled at him, with gratitude for each and every nutcase at the table. It was likely the only sincere smile I'd ever offered him. "Yes," I said. "We sure do."

I got up to go wash my hands.

Recipes...

Mamma's Standard Dressing

Ingredients:

1 cup (2 sticks) unsalted butter plus some for the baking dish

1 loaf good-quality day old Italian or French bread torn into 1-inch pieces (about 6 cups)

1 loaf good-quality sourdough, torn into 1-inch pieces (about 6 cups)

1 chopped sweet onion

3 minced shallots

1 cup chopped scallions

1/2 cup minced leek, white and pale green parts only

1 3/4 cups chopped celery

3/4 cup chopped fresh parsley or 2 tablespoons dried

1 tablespoon dried rosemary

1 1/2 teaspoons dried thyme

2 teaspoons ground savory

1 teaspoon dried marjoram

2 teaspoons kosher salt

1 teaspoon freshly ground black pepper

3 - 4 cups low-sodium chicken broth, divided

3 large eggs

*All herbs and seasonings should be adjusted to your individual taste.

Directions

1. Preheat oven to 250°.
2. Scatter bread in a single layer on two rimmed baking sheets.
3. Bake, stirring occasionally, until dried out with some golden-brown coloring, about 1 hour.
4. Let cool; transfer to a very large bowl.
5. Butter a large casserole dish. Mine is 14 x 11 (4 quarts) but you could use a 13 x 11.
6. Melt butter in a large skillet over medium-high heat; add onions, shallots, leeks, and celery. Stir often until just beginning to caramelize, about 15 minutes.
7. Add to bowl with bread.
8. Stir in herbs, salt, and pepper.
9. Drizzle in 2 cups broth and toss gently.
10. Let cool.
11. Whisk eggs in a small bowl.
12. Add 1 cup broth.
13. Fold gently into bread mixture until thoroughly combined.
14. Add additional broth if dressing seems too dry.
15. Transfer to buttered casserole dish.
16. Cover with foil and bake 40 minutes.
17. Uncover and bake until dressing is set and top is lightly browned and a bit crisp, about 45 minutes more unless you have other things in the oven. Then it might take longer.

* I make mine a day ahead, through step 15. I cover and refrig-

erate it, then take it out and let it sit on the counter for about 30 minutes before baking.

Mother's Day Squash Casserole

Ingredients:
  2 pounds yellow squash, sliced
  1 zucchini, sliced
  ½ cup shredded carrots
  1 cup green onions, sliced
  2 ounces diced pimentos (1/2 small jar)
  1/2 cup butter (1 stick)
  ½ cup sour cream
  ½ cup Duke's mayonnaise
  1 can cream of mushroom soup
  1 cup shredded Monterey Jack and Colby cheese blend
  4 slices of American cheese
  1 egg
  1 sleeve of saltines, crushed
  salt and pepper to taste
  French's fried onion rings for topping

Directions

1. Place squash, zucchini, and carrots in a medium saucepan and cook over medium heat until tender.
2. Remove from heat.
3. Place in a colander and let drain while making sauce. Drain very well and transfer to a bowl or the original saucepan.
4. Melt butter in a skillet.
5. Add onion and cook until tender.
6. Add mushroom soup, cheeses, sour cream, and mayonnaise.
7. Cook over low heat until well blended and smooth.
8. Beat egg and add to squash mixture.
9. Stir in pimento.
10. Add to sauce and blend everything well.
11. Add salt and pepper to taste.
12. Stir in crushed saltines.
13. Pour into a lightly greased casserole dish, top with French's onion rings and bake at 350° about 40 minutes, until bubbly and top is golden brown.

Makes 8 to 10 servings.

Cream Cheese & Olive Deviled Eggs

Ingredients:
12 hardboiled eggs, peeled
8 ounces cream cheese, softened
2 tablespoons olive juice
½ teaspoon salt
1 teaspoon coarse ground black pepper
2 tablespoon chopped dried chives
4 generously rounded tablespoons Duke's mayonnaise
24 green, pimento-stuffed olives

Directions

1. Cut eggs in half lengthwise, then scoop out yolks and add to softened cream cheese.
2. Place egg white halves on serving platter.
3. Add all remaining ingredients except olives to the cream cheese mixture.
4. Mix with hand mixer until smooth.
5. Stuff egg whites with cream cheese mixture.

6. Top each half egg with an olive.
7. Chill until ready to serve.

Mamma's Trifle

Ingredients:

Roughly half a cream cheese pound cake.
    Recipe follows. Once it's cool, cut about half of it into cubes.
(I slice and freeze what I don't use.)

Mamma's Vanilla Custard
    Recipe follows. (She also uses this in her banana pudding.)
Let it cool just a bit, but stir it occasionally.

Your favorite fresh fruits—I use strawberries, raspberries,
pineapple, and kiwi. Sometimes I just use strawberries and kiwi,
and other times I use just the berries. Use the fruits you like the
best. I typically use a couple pints of berries, a couple kiwi, and a
cup or so of the pineapple. This isn't an exact science.

Raspberry Glaze

Make this by melting a jar of seedless raspberry jam over low heat and adding 2-3 tablespoons of Chambord.

Sweetened whipped cream
    Recipe follows.

Assemble the trifle:

1. Drizzle some of the glaze on the sides of the trifle bowl —not much, just enough to make a few decorative swirls.
2. Layer cake cubes, custard, and fruit, drizzling a little glaze on after each layer. (If you need more cake, slice off another chunk and cube it as you need it.)
3. Top with sweetened whipped cream.

Cream Cheese Pound Cake

Ingredients:

*Bring all ingredients to room temperature before using.

1 1/2 cups butter (3 sticks)
1/3 cup sour cream
8 ounces cream cheese
2 teaspoons vanilla
3 cups cake flour
3 cups sugar
6 large eggs
1/8 teaspoon salt
1/2 teaspoon baking powder

Directions:

1. Beat butter and cream cheese until thoroughly blended.

2. Slowly add sugar. Mix for 5 to 7 minutes.
3. Add eggs, one at a time, mixing each time.Grease and flour a 10" tube pan.
4. Bake in a 300° pre-heated oven for 1 ¼ to 1 ½ hours.

Mamma's Vanilla Custard

Ingredients:
- 1 cup sugar
- 1/4 cup flour
- 1/8 teaspoon salt
- 3 egg yolks
- 2 cups half and half*
- 1 tablespoon butter
- 2 teaspoons vanilla

Directions:

1. Mix together the sugar, flour, and salt in a heavy saucepan.
2. Beat the egg yolks slightly, then mix with the half and half.
3. Whisk the egg and milk mixture into the dry ingredients in the pot over medium heat.
4. Bring to a boil, whisking constantly.
5. Let boil one minute, then remove from heat.
6. Stir in butter and vanilla until butter is melted.

7. Let cool slightly, stirring occasionally.

*The half and half is a subject of dissension in our family. This recipe originated with my mother, and she has used it as the basis for all her custards for years. SHE uses evaporated milk, 1 can, though the cans aren't the same size they used to be, and one can of water.

I like using two cups of half and half in mine, and have done this as long as I can remember. She maintains (as did HER mother) that it tastes better if you use evaporated milk. I tell you this so that you can decide for yourself. I'll say this, no one has ever turned down either of our custards. If you try it, let me know which way you did it and how it turned out.

Sweetened Whipped Cream

Ingredients:
    1/4 cup sugar
    2 tablespoons vanilla
    1 pint heavy whipping cream

Add ingredients to deep bowl and whip until stiff.

I so hope you've enjoyed these Liz Talbot short stories and the recipes! If you did, I'd love to see your thoughts in a review—if you're the review-leaving sort, of course. If you'd like to stay in touch and be notified about new releases, please sign up for my newsletter. Click the link below to go to my website, then scroll to the bottom on any page or wait for the pop-up. https://susanmboyer.com

Warmly,

. . .

Susan

About the Author

Susan M. Boyer is the author of the USA TODAY bestselling Liz Talbot mystery series. She was blessed with a quintessential small-town childhood and has had a life-long love affair with books. Susan is grateful to have been gifted with an over-active imagination. She was one of those children whose teachers were always telling her mamma that her talents needed to be "channeled." She's been making things up and writing them down her whole life.

Susan's debut novel, *Lowcountry Boil*, won the 2012 Agatha Award for Best First Novel, the Daphne du Maurier Award for Excellence in Mystery/Suspense, and garnered several other award nominations. The third book in the series, *Lowcountry Boneyard*, was a Spring 2015 Southern Independent Booksellers Alliance (SIBA) Okra Pick, and was short-listed for the 2016 Pat Conroy Beach Music Mystery Prize.

Lowcountry Book Club was a Summer 2016 SIBA Okra Pick

and was short-listed for the 2017 Southern Book Prize in Mystery & Detective Fiction.

There are currently ten books in the Liz Talbot Series. Liz Talbot and Nate Andrews will have a new case in 2022.

Susan loves beaches, Southern food, and small Southern towns where everyone knows everyone, and everyone has crazy relatives. You'll find all of the above in her novels. She lives in North Carolina with her husband, and spends every second she can on the Carolina coast.

Susan loves to hear from readers. You can reach her through her website: https://www.susanmboyer.com/

Sign up for her newsletter on any page of her website (scroll to the bottom or wait for the pop-up) to get recipes from her books and to be among the first to hear the news when the next book is scheduled for release.

Also by Susan M. Boyer

Lowcountry Boil (A Liz Talbot Mystery, Book 1)

Lowcountry Bombshell (A Liz Talbot Mystery, Book 2)

Lowcountry Boneyard (A Liz Talbot Mystery, Book 3)

Lowcountry Bordello (A Liz Talbot Mystery, Book 4)

Lowcountry Book Club (A Liz Talbot Mystery, Book 5)

Lowcountry Bonfire (A Liz Talbot Mystery, Book 6)

Lowcountry Bookshop (A Liz Talbot Mystery, Book 7)

Lowcountry Boomerang (A Liz Talbot Mystery, Book 8)

Lowcountry Boondoggle (A Liz Talbot Mystery, Book 9)

Lowcountry Boughs of Holly (A Liz Talbot Mystery, Book 10)

Coming Soon! Lowcountry Getaway (A Liz Talbot Mystery, Book 11)